To Tony
—M.K

Aberdeenshire Library and Information Service
www.aberdeenshire.gov.uk/libraries
Renewals Hotline 01224 661511

KELLY, Mij

The happiest man in the world, or,
The mouse who made Christmas

The
HAPPIEST
Man in the World

Written by
Mij Kelly

Illustrated by
Louise Nisbet

First published in 2008
by Hodder Children's Books

This PB edition published in 2009

Text copyright © Mij Kelly 2008
Illustration copyright © Louise Nisbet 2008

Hodder Children's Books
338 Euston Road
London NW1 3BH

Hodder Children's Books Australia
Level 17/207 Kent Street
Sydney, NSW 2000

A catalogue record of this book is available
from the British Library.

ISBN: 978 0 340 93155 4
10 9 8 7 6 5 4 3 2 1

Printed in China

Hodder Children's Books is a division
of Hachette Children's Books.
An Hachette UK Company
www.hachette.co.uk

Written by
Mij Kelly

Illustrated by
Louise Nisbet

The
HAPPIEST
Man *in the* World
or the mouse who made Christmas

Hodder
Children's
Books

A division of Hachette Children's Books

Mouse lived in a narrow house

crammed between a lot
of other houses. She lived
on her own, except for
a few spiders and beetles –
and that's how she liked it.
Mouse didn't like people.
She didn't like anyone.

Every day she helped herself to bread from
the baker, pork pies from the butcher and
treats from the deli.

Every night she had a feast. Sometimes
the beetles would gather round and gaze
at her with their strange beetle eyes.

'Get lost,' said Mouse. 'Why should I give
you anything?'

One autumn day she came home with a choice slice of gorgonzola under one arm. There was an old man with a suitcase in the hall.

'Excuse me,' said Mouse. 'But this is MY house.'
'I'm pretty sure it's mine,' said the old man. 'Because I've just bought it. But stay if you want. I don't care.'

He carried his suitcase
into the front room and
put it down.

'Once upon a time
I was the happiest man
in the world,' he said.
'Now look at me.'

Everything about the old man
was dismal and grey.
'Give, give, give,' he sighed.
'That's all I've ever done.
But I can't see the
point any more.'

'That's because there is no point,'
said Mouse, who had never given
anybody anything in her life.
  And then she thought. 'At least
now there's a human in the house
I won't have to go out in the cold.
I'll just help myself to whatever's
in the fridge.'

  But the old man never went
out of the house. He didn't
unpack his suitcase. He just sat
by the window and stared.

Winter came and there was nothing
to look at but grey streets, bare trees
and a sky that glowered with snow.

'Don't you ever eat?' asked Mouse.
'I'm too sad to eat,' said the old
man and took to his bed.
'Please get up,' said Mouse.
'I can't,' said the old man. 'I think
my heart is broken.'
'Oh please!' thought Mouse.
'I am so sick of hearing this!'

Living with the old man was like living under a gloomy grey cloud. Mouse was thinking this one day as she sneaked around the deli – and right at that moment she spotted a clementine, bright and orange and full of good cheer.

'That clementine is just what I need to cheer myself up,' thought Mouse. And then she thought, 'Maybe it's just what I need to cheer up the sad old man who's making me miserable.'

So she carried the clementine home and
gave it to the old man, who was still lying
in bed.

'Is that for me?' he whispered, as if he
could hardly believe someone might give
him a present.

'Yes,' said Mouse, and the old man's ears
turned pink. He took the clementine,
he ate it and he said "thank you".

'Well that's a bit better,'
thought Mouse.

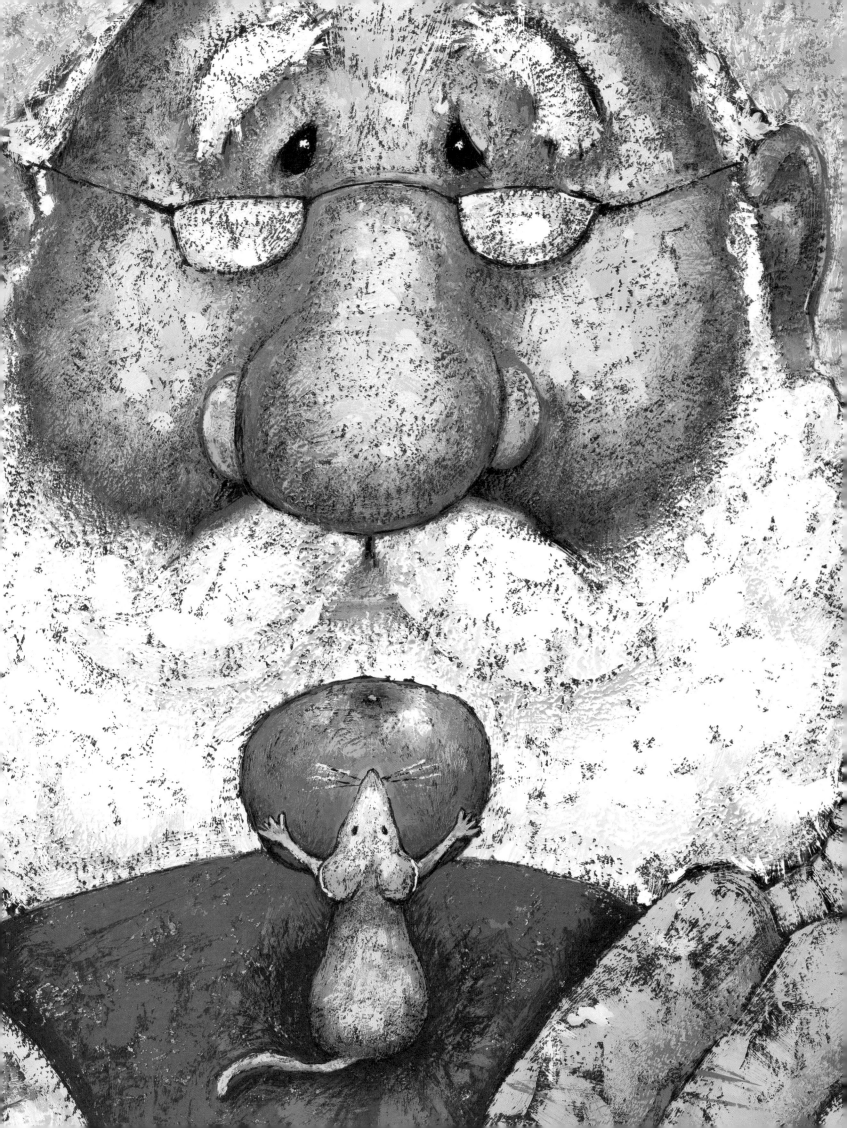

The next day, there was frost on the windows and the old man still wouldn't get out of bed.

But that afternoon, when Mouse was sneaking around the baker's shop, she spotted a mince pie.

It was so fat and fruity, bursting at
the seams like generosity itself, that Mouse
decided to take it home for the old man.

'Is that for me?' he asked.

'Yes,' said Mouse, and the tip of the old man's
nose turned pink with pleasure.
He took the mince pie and he ate it.
He almost smiled when he said "thank you".

'Now that,' thought Mouse, 'is a great
deal better.'

The next day the sky was
as blue as only a blue sky
can be. As for the world,
it had turned white.
But the old man wouldn't
even get out of bed
to look out of the
window.

When Mouse went outside
she slithered in snow and
scrabbled on ice and the tip
of her nose turned blue
with cold.

By the time she reached
the butcher's, the shop was
closed. She had to sneak
under the door.

Mouse couldn't believe it. Everything had
been sold. There was nothing on the shelves
but useless old tinsel.

She stared at the tinsel for a long time and,
at last, she saw that it was full of shimmers
and surprises, just like Christmas.

'I brought you a present to brighten
the room,' said Mouse.

'Is it Christmas?' asked the old man,
and he looked more miserable than ever.

'It's Christmas Eve,' said Mouse,
'but I'm giving you your present now.'
    'A Christmas present?' asked the old man.
'For me?'
    He took the tinsel and wrapped it round
his head like a crown. 'Thank you,' he said
and he smiled.

Mouse was so pleased she danced across
the coverlet and clapped her hands.
'I made you smile!' she crowed.

By now the old man's face was so pink
that his beard looked quite white.
'It's a wonderful feeling when you make
someone smile,' he said. 'It's the best
feeling in the world, don't you think?'
'Of course it is,' said Mouse, who could
see that now.
'Of course it is!' exclaimed the old man.
'How could I have forgotten?'

He leapt out of bed,
opened his suitcase and
put on his clothes.

It was like pulling a cracker when he whistled for
his reindeer and like fireworks and rockets when
the reindeer arrived.

Safe in his pocket, Mouse saw everything.
She saw prancing hooves on a snow-covered roof.
She saw shimmers and snowdrifts.
She saw sack-loads of gifts. And then
she was flying high in the sky
and the stars looked like
snowflakes, the snowflakes
like stars.

She could hear people singing and far-off bells ringing, but the best of it was when she was delivering presents, sneaking down chimneys, stuffing stockings with toys.

That was a joy.

'I think I must be the happiest mouse
in the world,' said Mouse.

The happiest man
in the world just laughed.